RED SQUIRREL CROSSING

By
Selassie I. Fox

Published by BroHawk Productions LLC

Photography by Selassie Fox
Art Animation:
Selassie Fox & Monique Momrelle &
Gregory Daley

ISBN: 978-0-9987561-0-3

www.BroHawk.com/RSC

G GENERAL
AUDIENCES

All Ages Admitted

Once upon a time on the Isle of Man
two grey squirrels named Ferdinand and
Isabella lived in a tree overlooking the
Irish Sea.

Ferdinand: Home sweet home.

Isabella: I suppose this will do for now.

The Isle of Man is where Ferdinand and Isabella would call their home. They lived there in harmony with many other grey squirrels and black and brown squirrels.

Ferdinand: I'm glad I have this coat now that I'm North.

Isabella: Me too. You know, it's not so bad being a squirrel.

Now Ferdinand and Isabella were special squirrels because they were the only squirrels living on Isle of Man that swam there from another country.

Isabella: I was a child riding the ferry when I saw this enchanted island. I always wanted to live here.

Ferdinand and Isabella remembered life beyond the waves of the Irish Sea where they were born. Unlike the other squirrels, whose ancestors were born on the Isle of Man.

Ferdinand: That was epic! Honestly I could've swum to Scotland if Isabella asked me.

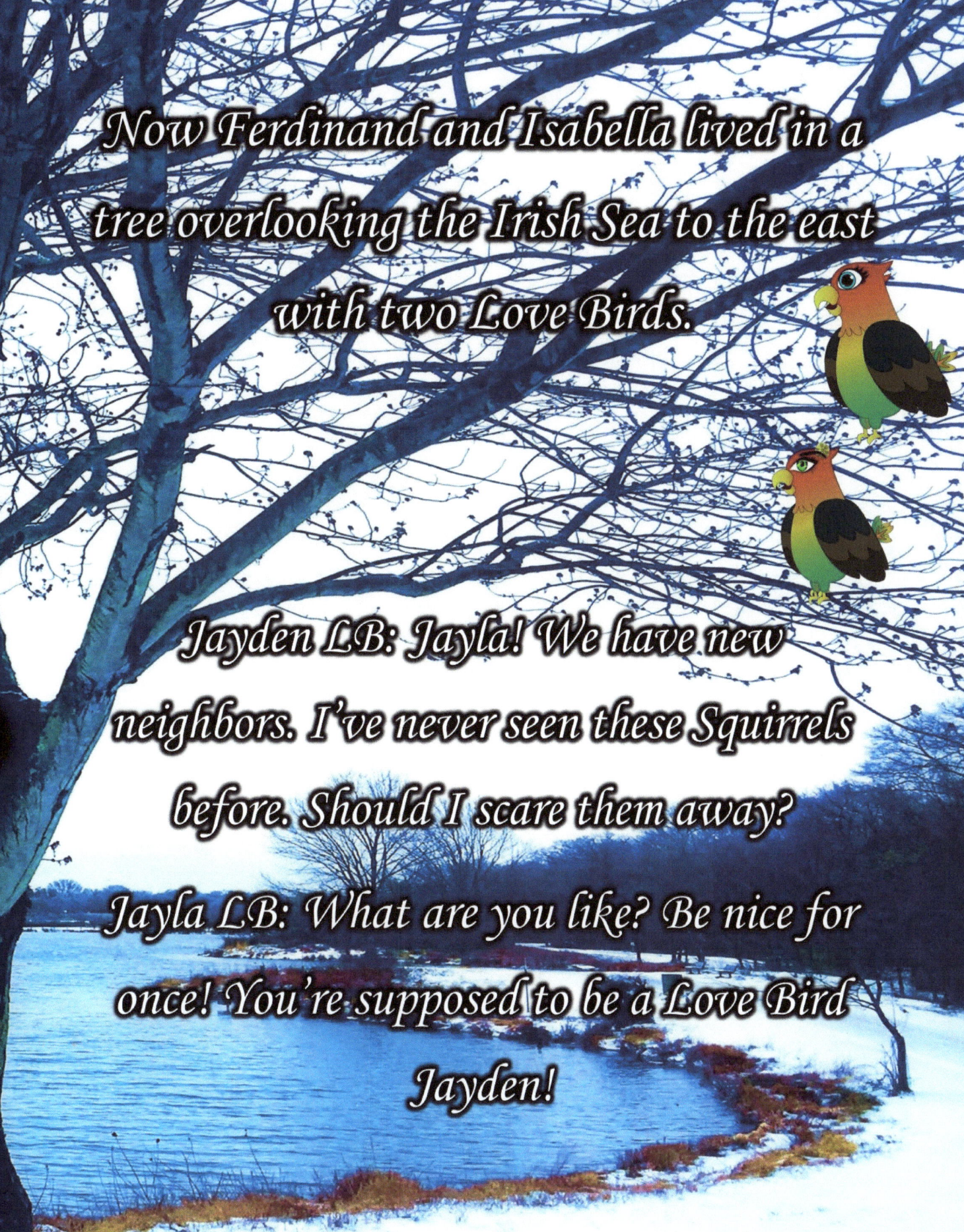

Now Ferdinand and Isabella lived in a tree overlooking the Irish Sea to the east with two Love Birds.

Jayden LB: Jayla! We have new neighbors. I've never seen these Squirrels before. Should I scare them away?

Jayla LB: What are you like? Be nice for once! You're supposed to be a Love Bird Jayden!

During the cold winter nights they cuddled to keep warm.

Isabella: I love you honey.

Ferdinand: I love you too darling.

Then one spring night, the moon became red and Isabella had a baby boy with red hair.

Ferdinand: Congratulations Isabella, now you're a Mother.

Isabella: And you're a Father.

Ferdinand: I'll be the best Father.

Isabella: And I'll be the best Mother.

All the squirrels and birds gathered to see the first red squirrel on the island of trees.

Ferdinand: Thanks for coming everyone. Isabella and the baby are doing well.

Then the Love Birds looked to Ferdinand and Isabella and said, "What's his name?" And Ferdinand picked up his son, and said "My son shall be named Ian."

Jayden LB: Typical Scottish name. Fitting for an extraordinary red squirrel.

All the squirrels and birds sang and celebrated the miraculous birth of Ian under the red moon.

Jayla LB: Aww, I haven't seen everyone this happy in many years.

Jayden LB: Yes Love, but I do hope everyone would clean up before they leave.

The next morning Ian had many visitors who came to see the red squirrel born under the red moon.

Isabella: Hi everyone, Ian just woke up. Come and meet my baby boy.

The wise old brown squirrel who also lived in the community of trees said Ian's birth was, "A sign beyond the clouds."

Jayden LB: My word, that old brown squirrel always has his head in the clouds.

Many other young squirrels wanted to play with Ian, so their tree had many visitors all day long.

Ferdinand: Isabella, it looks like our son is becoming the most popular squirrel on the Isle of Man.

Ferdinand stayed by Ian's side and showed him how to climb the trees so he could explore the beautiful enchanted Isle of Man.

Isabella: Ferdinand, don't let Ian go too far. He has to eat soon.

He learned how to talk and run and jump between the branches.

Ian: Thanks Dad for teaching me how to climb. Can I learn how to fly tomorrow?

Ferdinand: We're not flying squirrels son. Don't think about it!

Ferdinand taught Ian how to tell the difference between good and bad nuts by holding them in his paws.

Ian: Dad! I found a hazelnut with a ladybug on it! Can I eat the ladybug too?

Ferdinand: No son, you should never eat a lady bug. They protect our trees so please treat them with respect.

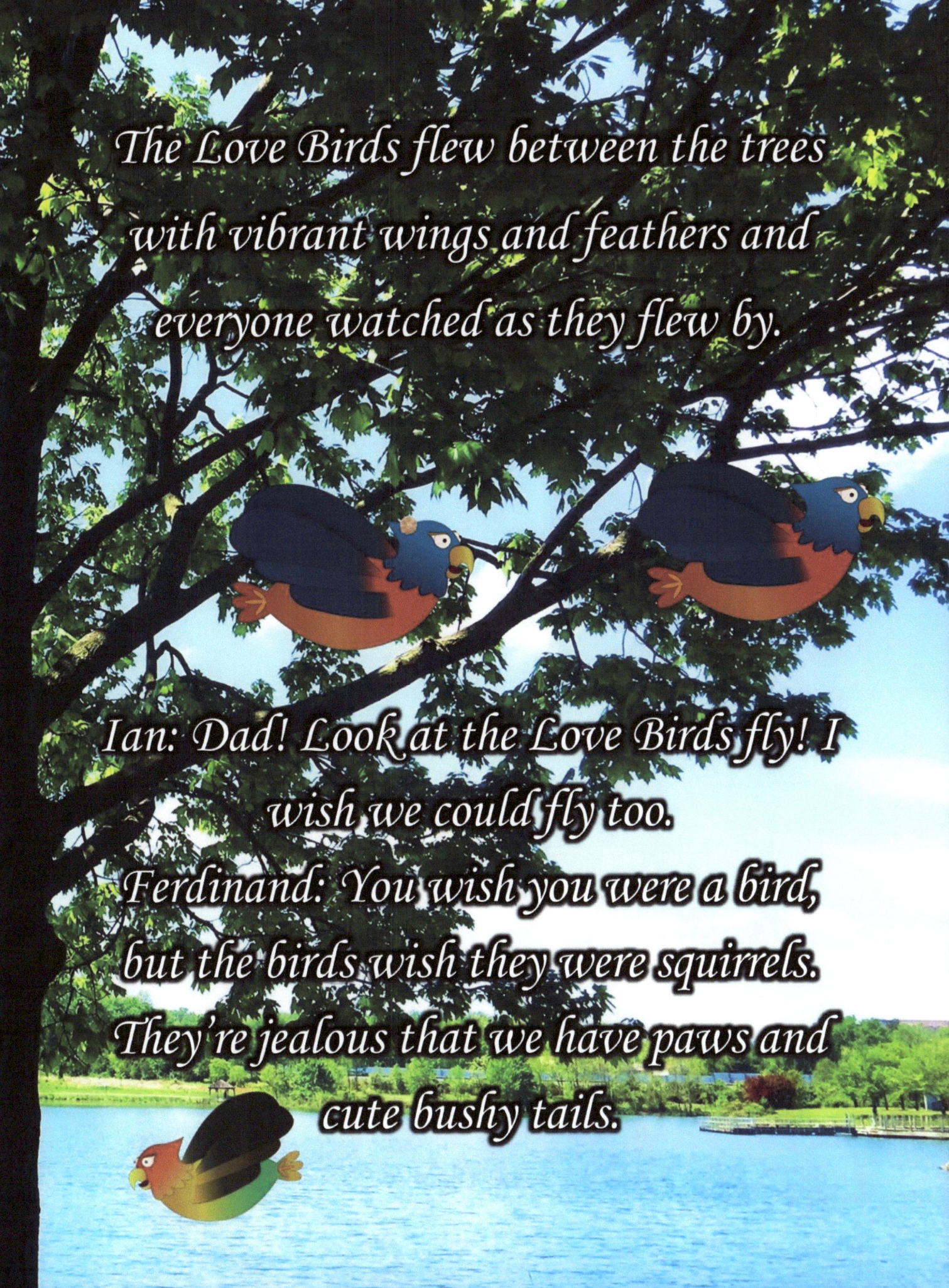

The Love Birds flew between the trees with vibrant wings and feathers and everyone watched as they flew by.

Ian: Dad! Look at the Love Birds fly! I wish we could fly too.

Ferdinand: You wish you were a bird, but the birds wish they were squirrels. They're jealous that we have paws and cute bushy tails.

As time passed, Ian grew to be faster and stronger than the other squirrels. Jealousy and envy amongst the grey, brown and black squirrels would test Ian's character.

Ian raced with the other squirrels through the trees and he collected the most food. As Ian won the race all the girls cheered for him.

Ian: Yes! I won! I'm the fastest squirrel on the Isle of Man!

After Ian won the race, Morgan came to Ian to congratulate him. Then she confessed her love for Ian.

Although Morgan loved Ian, she sadly said, "I've never liked a red squirrel before." And she was scared of what other squirrels would think of her, so she said, "Let's just be friends."

When Ian got home he told his parents. But Ferdinand and Isabella tried to explain race relations in an intellectual way and Ian did not understand.

Ian: How come you're grey and I'm red?

Ferdinand: You see son, God lives in the clouds. And sometimes there's thunder and rain.

Isabella: Ian, I think what your father is trying to say is, long time ago we evolved from germs in the ocean, and...

Ferdinand: God made us in all shapes and colors. Some are fast like you and some are slow like that old brown squirrel who carries a stick to walk.

Then Ian turned to the Love Birds who live in his tree for friendship.

Ian: How did you learn to fly?

Jayla LB: I just flapped my wings and I began to fly since I was a baby bird still in my parent's nest.

Jayden LB: Quite the contrary for me, Ian. I knew how to fly before I hatched from my egg.

The Love Birds played games with Ian and gave him advice on where to find things that are far away.

Jayden LB: Ian! I found some Yorkshire pudding and crumpets in the park.

Jayla LB: Ian! I saw a tree full of hazel nuts that none of the other squirrels have touched.

The Love Birds also brought gifts for Ian just to make him smile.

Jayla LB: Ring the bell for tea Jayden. You are welcome to join us Ian.

Jayden LB: Hey Ian, would you like some tea and biscuits?

Ian: Thanks! You're the best friends a red squirrel could ask for. I'm glad we live in the same tree.

When winter approached again, the Love Birds told Ian and his parents they were leaving the Isle of Man to stay with family overseas.

Jayla LB: We'll be back in the first week of Spring.

Isabella: Safe travels!

Ferdinand: Send us a post card!

Ian: Hey Jayden, could I ride on your back? I'm not very heavy and can help out with your nest when we arrive.

Isabella: No Ian.

Before the Love Birds left, Jayden told
Ian, "Many red squirrels live where
we're going. They even have a picture
sign of a red squirrel and people drive
slow just to see it."

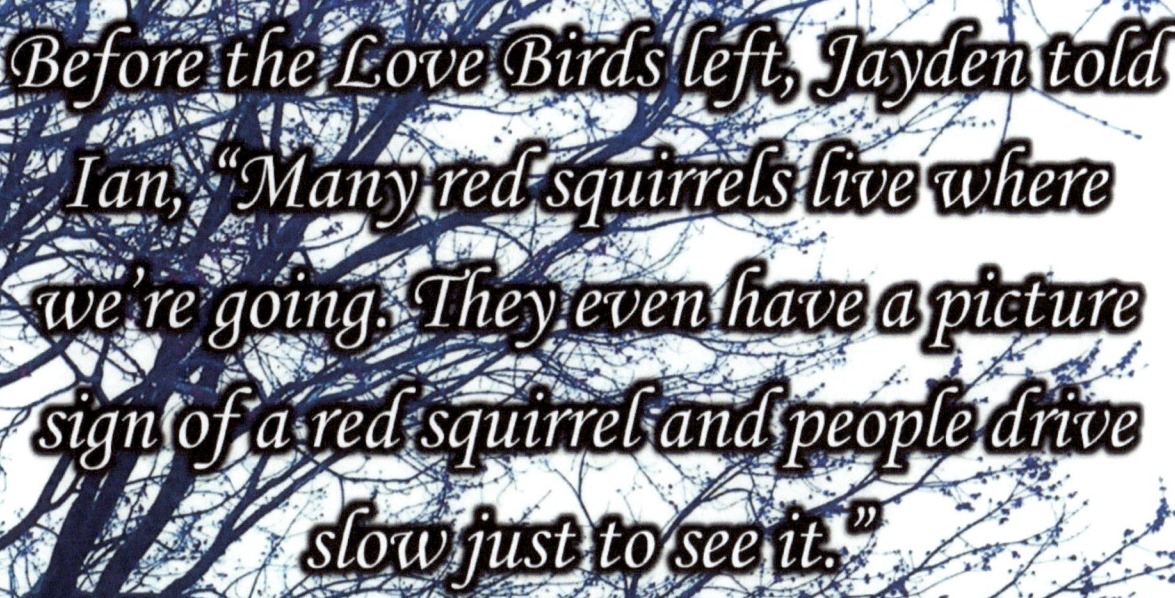

Jayla LB: Don't tempt Ian. That would
be quite a dangerous journey.

Jayden LB: Ian! There's a whole other
world out there. I could fly low and
show you the way.

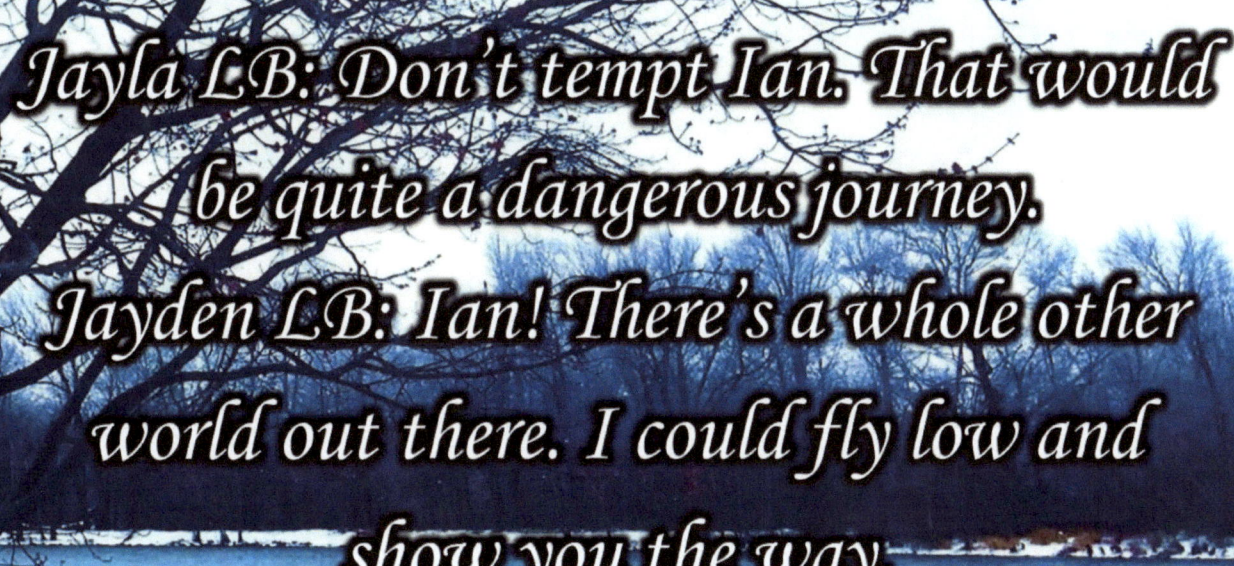

Ian would have to cross the frozen Irish Sea to join Jayden and Layla.

Ian: Wow! That sounds like a thrilling adventure. I could be the first squirrel to run across the ice.

Ian was excited for the challenge, but he didn't want his parents to worry, so he stayed home with Ferdinand and Isabella for the winter while the Love Birds flew away.

Jayden LB: Stay warm!

Jayla LB: See you next Spring!

That winter, Ian grew much closer to Ferdinand and Isabella.

Ian: Mom, tell me about the time when you and Dad swam to Isle of Man from Spain.

Ferdinand and Isabella told Ian stories of their past home and their journey swimming in the Sea to the Isle of Man. And Ian helped around the tree to keep everyone warm.

Isabella: I fear we swam for quite a number of days until we saw a very agreeable island past the English Channel called Hugh Town. But there wasn't anything for us to eat there. So we swam more in the Celtic Sea and up the Saint George's Channel into the Irish Sea.

Ferdinand: When your mother and I saw the Isle of Man we knew this would be our new home.

After the snow melted, Ferdinand and Isabella told Ian that next winter he will be old enough to go to Squirrel University at the Lake District National Park Campus.

Isabella: Ian, I know you're big, but you will always be my baby boy.

Ferdinand: Don't worry Isabella, Ian is smart and will learn from the best.

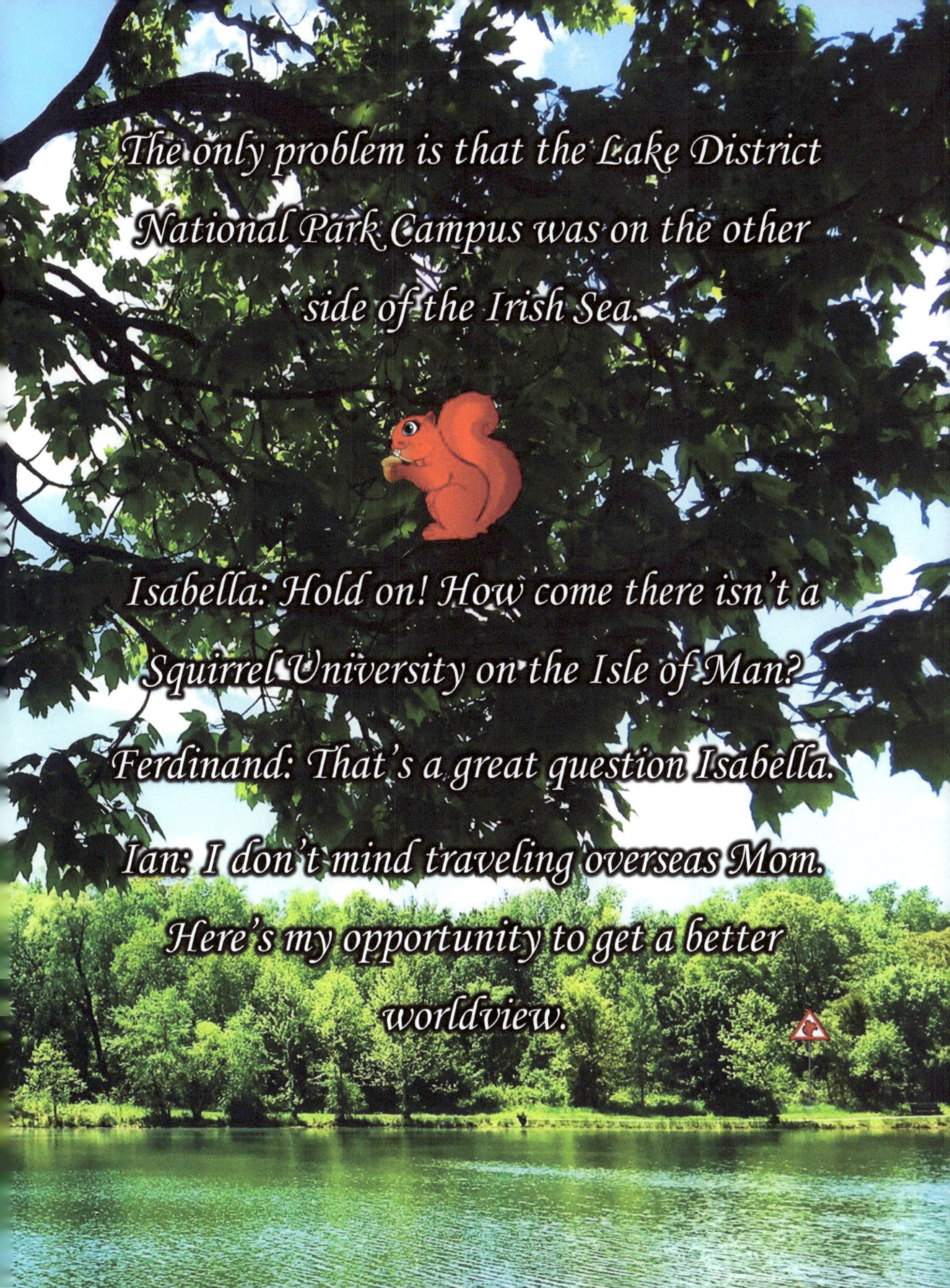

The only problem is that the Lake District National Park Campus was on the other side of the Irish Sea.

Isabella: Hold on! How come there isn't a Squirrel University on the Isle of Man?

Ferdinand: That's a great question Isabella.

Ian: I don't mind traveling overseas Mom. Here's my opportunity to get a better worldview.

As the Spring flowers bloomed, the Love Birds returned with good news for Ian.

Jayden LB: Ian! We've returned from spending time with family overseas. How has our nest been while we've been away?

Ian: A Pigeon from Ireland came and said he was your cousin on your father's side. He should still be there now.

All summer and fall, Ian played with the Love Birds throughout the trees on the Isle of Man. All the way up to the next winter storm.

Isabella: My son, hear the instruction of your father, and do not forsake the law of your mother and do your very best.

Ferdinand: Make me proud son! Listen to Jayden and Jayla when you're crossing the ice. And if sinners entice you, do not consent.

Ian: Thanks Mom and Dad! I love you both. I will remember everything you taught me and make you proud.

When the Sea became frozen, Ian and the Love Birds prepared to cross the Irish Sea.

Jayla LB: Ian, are you ready?

Ian: I was born ready!

Jayden LB: May the power of the wind guide us over the ice to fly with the moon.

The Love Birds prepared a home for Ian on the other side, and flew very low to guide him along the way.

Jayla LB: Watch out for that soft ice!

Ian's journey was an hour and a half of running across the frozen Sea and full of adventure.

Jayden LB: I could run faster if I were a squirrel.

Ian: And I could fly faster if I were a bird.

Slips and falls, soft ice and cold water would not be enough to stop Ian from crossing the Irish Sea.

Jayla LB: Watch out for that hole. Can you swim?

Jayden LB: Be careful Ian, if you fall in the freezing ocean, the sharks will eat you for dinner. They have sharp teeth. I've seen them eat bigger squirrels than you!

Ian: Those sharks swimming down there can't climb a tree faster than me. I'm the coolest squirrel in the United Kingdom!

Ian ran until the Love Birds told him

they're almost there.

Ian: How much further?

Jayden LB: Almost there Ian! You can

do it

When Ian saw the red squirrel crossing sign, he knew they arrived at his new home.

Ian: Whoa! That squirrel looks just like me!

Jayden LB: I told you Ian! Even the air smells sweeter over here!

Then the Love Birds showed Ian to his new house where he slept that night to get out of the cold snow.

Ian: Please tell my parents that I made it safely.

Jayla LB: Don't worry, Jayden is flying back tomorrow and will deliver your message to Ferdinand and Isabella.

Jayden LB: I am?

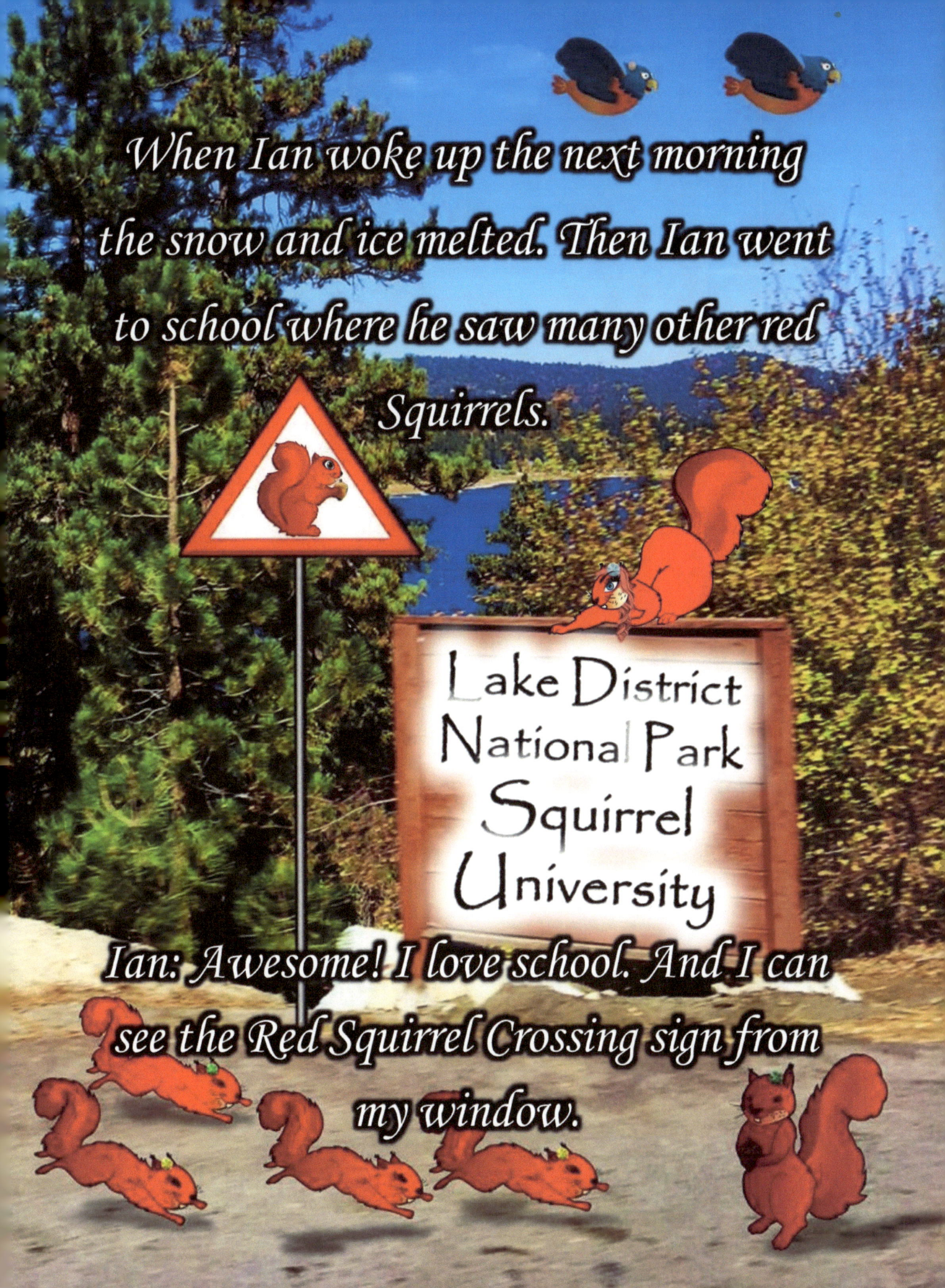

When Ian woke up the next morning the snow and ice melted. Then Ian went to school where he saw many other red Squirrels.

Lake District National Park Squirrel University

Ian: Awesome! I love school. And I can see the Red Squirrel Crossing sign from my window.

Ian introduced himself to his class, and everyone was surprised to learn he crossed the Irish Sea.

Ian: Hi everyone! My name is Ian, and I just moved here last night from the Isle of Man. It's a pleasure to meet you.

Many other squirrels introduced themselves except one grumpy red squirrel, and Ian felt happy again.

Ian: I have more friends here than I do at my parents' house. But I wish my parents could have crossed the ice with me.

The last Squirrel to introduce herself to the class said, "Hello everyone. My name is Emma." And Ian fell in love at first sight.

Ian: Wow! She is the most beautiful squirrel I've ever seen in my whole life.

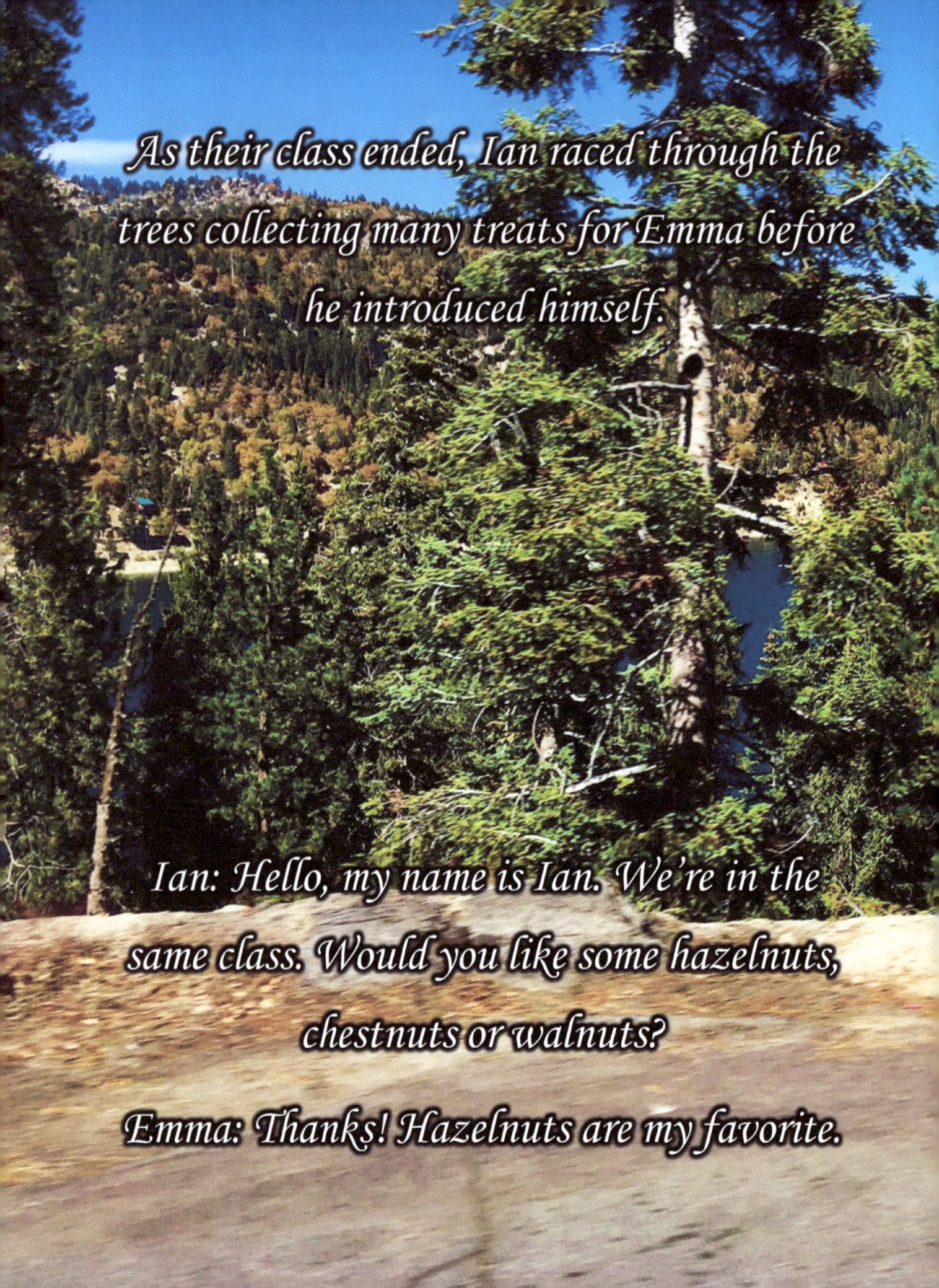

As their class ended, Ian raced through the trees collecting many treats for Emma before he introduced himself.

Ian: Hello, my name is Ian. We're in the same class. Would you like some hazelnuts, chestnuts or walnuts?

Emma: Thanks! Hazelnuts are my favorite.

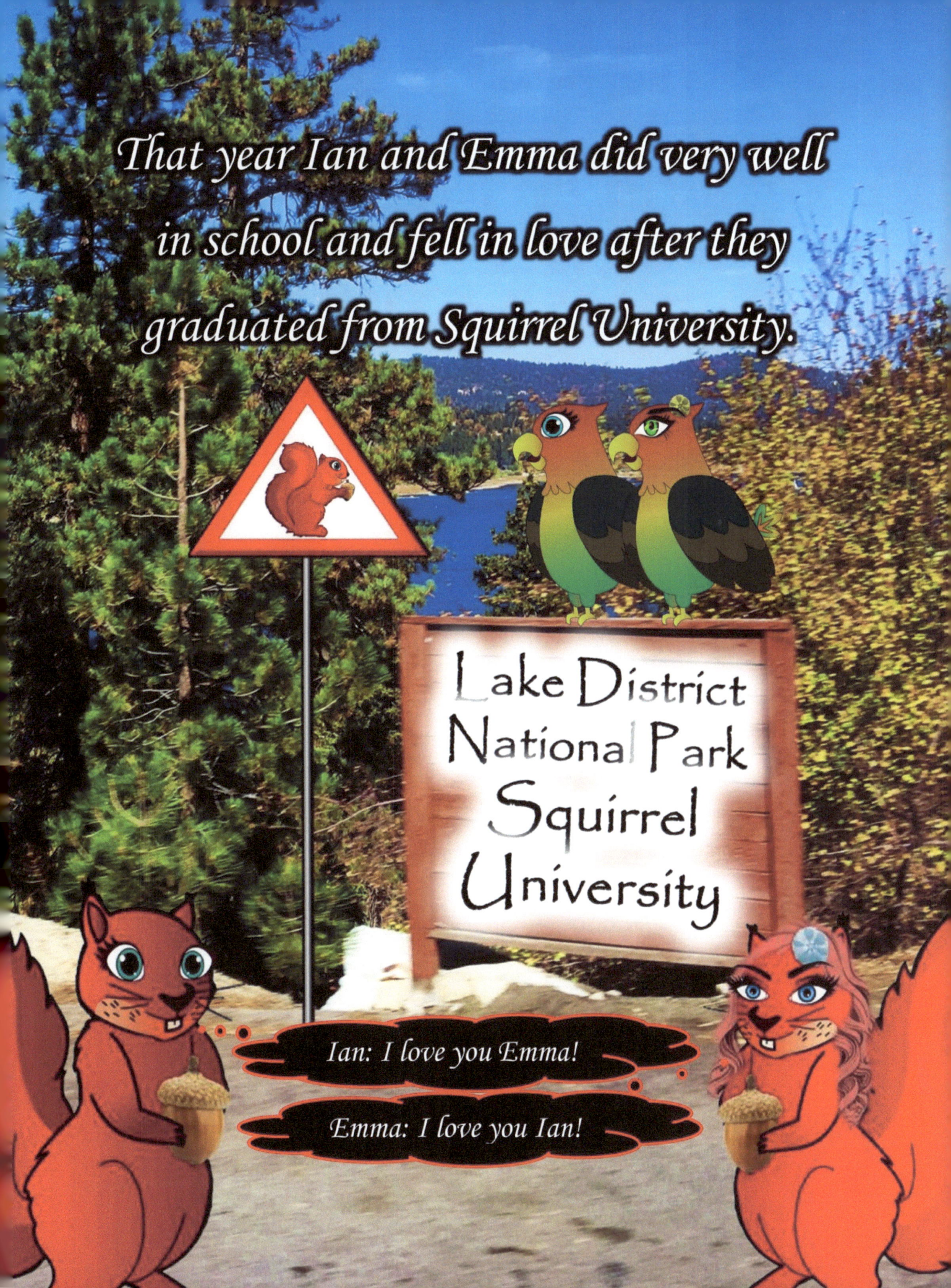

Ian and Emma lived happily ever after.

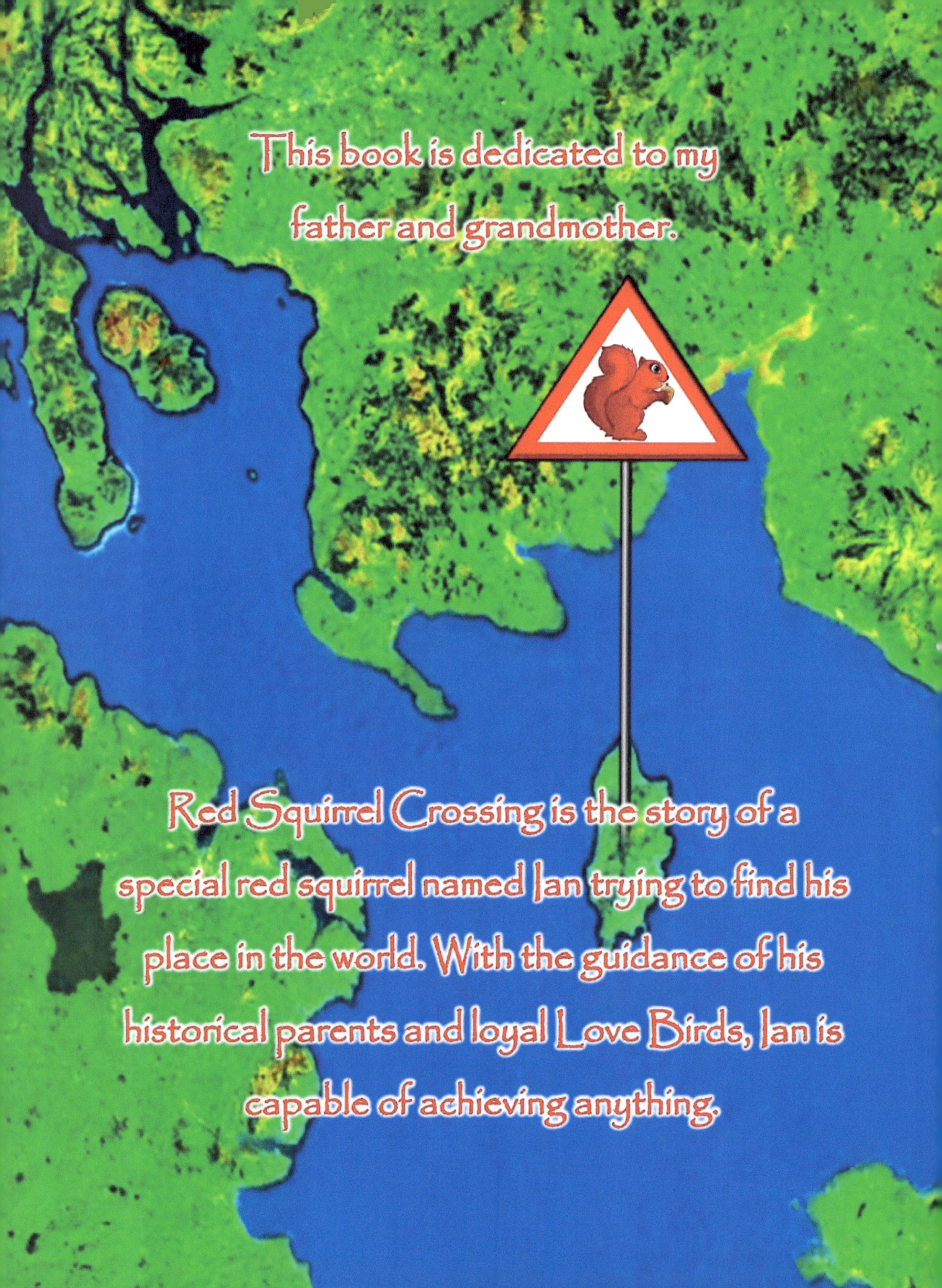

This book is dedicated to my father and grandmother.

Red Squirrel Crossing is the story of a special red squirrel named Ian trying to find his place in the world. With the guidance of his historical parents and loyal Love Birds, Ian is capable of achieving anything.

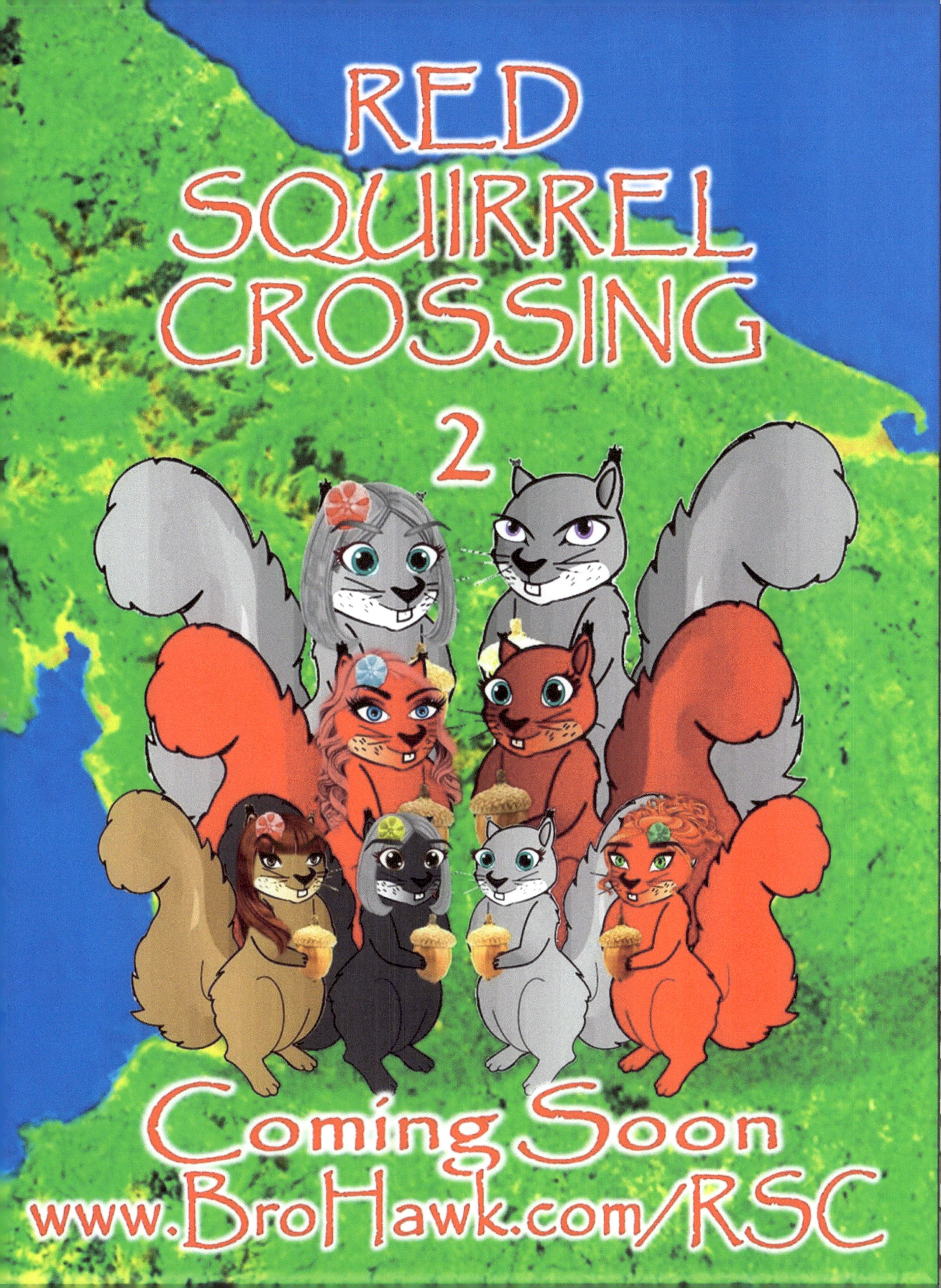

RED SQUIRREL CROSSING

2

Coming Soon

www.BroHawk.com/RSC